A
PUSSYCAT'S
CHRISTMAS

A
PUSSYCAT'S
CHRISTMAS

MARGARET WISE BROWN
ILLUSTRATED BY
ANNE MORTIMER

 KATHERINE TEGEN BOOKS
An Imprint of HarperCollins Publishers

IT was Christmas. How could you tell?
    Was the snow falling?
        No.
The little cat Pussycat knew that
    Christmas was coming.
The ice tinkled when it broke on the
    frozen mud puddles.
The cold air made her hair
    stand straight up in the air.
And the air smelled just as it did last year.

    What did it smell like?
Could she smell Christmas trees?

    Of course she could.

AND tangerines?
And Christmas greens?
And holly?
And could she hear the crackle and slip
of white tissue paper?
And red tissue paper?

She certainly could.

Tissue paper rustled.
Nuts cracked.
Scissors cut.

*B*RRRRRR.
There wasn't a flake of snow in the sky.
But the sky was dark and low,
and there was the dark smell of winter air
before snow.
And then,
click,
the street lights clicked on all over town.

And as the heavens turned dark
beyond the window,
one
by
one

the snowflakes began to fall out of the sky.

How did little Pussycat know?
Could she hear the snow?

S SHSHHHHHHHHSSSS.
    She certainly could.
And she ran right out into the snowstorm.
    For if there was anything
that this little cat loved,
    it was the cold, dry, fresh, white,
wild, and feathery, powdery snow.

She went pouncing around in it,
    bouncing around in joy.
And she ate some of it.
    And she rolled in it and dug in it
    and played with it.

And then she stood up all white
    with snow—
    very still.
For it was very quiet,
very quiet.

FIRST there was no sound.
And then there was some.
For when everything is quiet,
you can hear things far away.
From the sky with a sound
like steady whispering
came the snow—that sound of snow.

Then the wind rattled the black branches,
and rattled it was time for Pussycat
to go into the house.

For little cats do not like the wind.
They usually don't like snow,
but this little cat did.

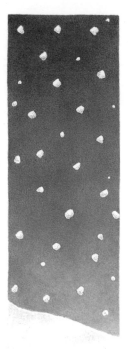

A̲ᴌᴌ the smells of the earth that she knew
were frozen and buried
in the white snow.
The world was very quiet and very mysterious.
Even footsteps were quiet.
Pussycat didn't go in right away
because through the wind and the falling snow
she heard something.

She stood very still and stretched her ears
there in the whitened
darkness.
And soon she heard it
coming from far away,
away up the snowy road.

Ding, ding, ding, ding,

Jingle, jingle jingle, ding.

What was it?
She heard it going by
in the white falling snow.

SHE saw it!
She saw the sleigh go jingling by.

THEN Pussycat meowed at her windowpane.
And she heard footsteps coming to let her in.
They always let her in right away
because they didn't want her to get cold
and they liked to have her in the house.

She walked right into the living room
where she could smell the sharp tangy smell
of the Christmas tree and candles
and nuts and raisins
and apples and tangerines.

But they shouldn't have let her stay
in the living room
where they were wrapping up packages
and hanging things on the tree.

AND this is why.
Pussycat pounced.
She pounced on everything.
And she waited to pounce with shining eyes
and switching tail.

She waited with shining eyes
for something to fall,
to tinkle, to crash, and to break.

She batted the Christmas tree balls
with her paw.
Tore at the tissue paper
and pulled the bows off
the packages.

So they put her out
in the hall
and closed the
glass doors.

PUSSYCAT lay down and purred by the fire.
She lifted her ears and she listened.
There was a sound of crackling.
Shhhhh, shhhhh, crackle.
What was that? Was it the fire?

Always there was the sound of snow
hissing against the windowpane.

There was a tiny tinkle little *pop*,
as something fell from the Christmas tree
and shivered into a million splinters of light.
That was wonderful.

The lights gleamed in Pussycat's eyes.
Then

bang, bang, bang.

What was that?
Someone was hanging
the Christmas stockings.

Everyone came out and stepped over
and around the little cat
and put on coats and boots
and mufflers and hats
and laughed and shuffled about.

They kissed each other under the mistletoe.
Then off they went to church.

Suddenly and quietly far off in the night
Pussycat could hear

Ding dong, ding dong, ding dong, ding dong.

When everyone had gone
it was dark and quiet.
The snow had stopped.
And there was only the smell
of the Christmas tree
filling the house.
And silence.

THEN softly at first but distinct in the night
    she heard people walking
from window to window—
    the dark carolers on the white snow.

Through the still air their voices
    came to her listening ears—
over the silence of the frozen snow—
    in the silence of the moonlight—
in the silence of the night—
    in the silence of the bright stars
      high in the sky:

Silent Night, Holy Night, All is calm, All is bright . . .

And as the little Pussycat
    purred and purred by the fire,
she heard in the distance
    the music fading far down the road.

THEN she pushed open
the living room door with her paw
and there in the silent house
was the Christmas tree.
It sparkled and glistened with lights,
gold and silver and blue,
the light of rubies and emeralds,
shining like no tree that any cat
had ever seen in the woods.

THIS to Pussycat was Christmas Eve.

For Tyler
—A.M.

The illustrations in this book were painted with watercolors on Archers Not paper.

Katherine Tegen Books is an imprint of HarperCollins Publishers.

A Pussycat's Christmas
Text copyright © 1949 by Margaret Wise Brown
Text copyright renewed 1977 by Roberta Brown Rauch
Illustrations copyright © 1994 by Anne Mortimer
All rights reserved. Manufactured in China.
No part of this book may be used or reproduced in any manner whatsoever without written
permission except in the case of brief quotations embodied in critical articles and reviews.
For information address HarperCollins Children's Books, a division of HarperCollins
Publishers, 10 East 53rd Street, New York, NY 10022.
www.harpercollinschildrens.com
Library of Congress Cataloging-in-Publication Data
Brown, Margaret Wise, 1910–1952.
A pussycat's Christmas / by Margaret Wise Brown ; paintings by Anne Mortimer.
p. cm.
Summary: Pussycat knows Christmas is coming, plays in the snow, and watches the Christmas preparations.
ISBN 978-0-06-186978-5
[1. Christmas—Fiction. 2. Cats—Fiction.] I. Mortimer, Anne, ill. II. Title. III. Title: Pussycat's Christmas.
PZ7.B816Pu 1994   93-4424   [E]—dc20   CIP   AC

09 10 11 12 13   SCP   10 9 8 7 6 5 4 3 2 1
❖
First paper-over-board edition, 2009